It was the end of
Book Week.

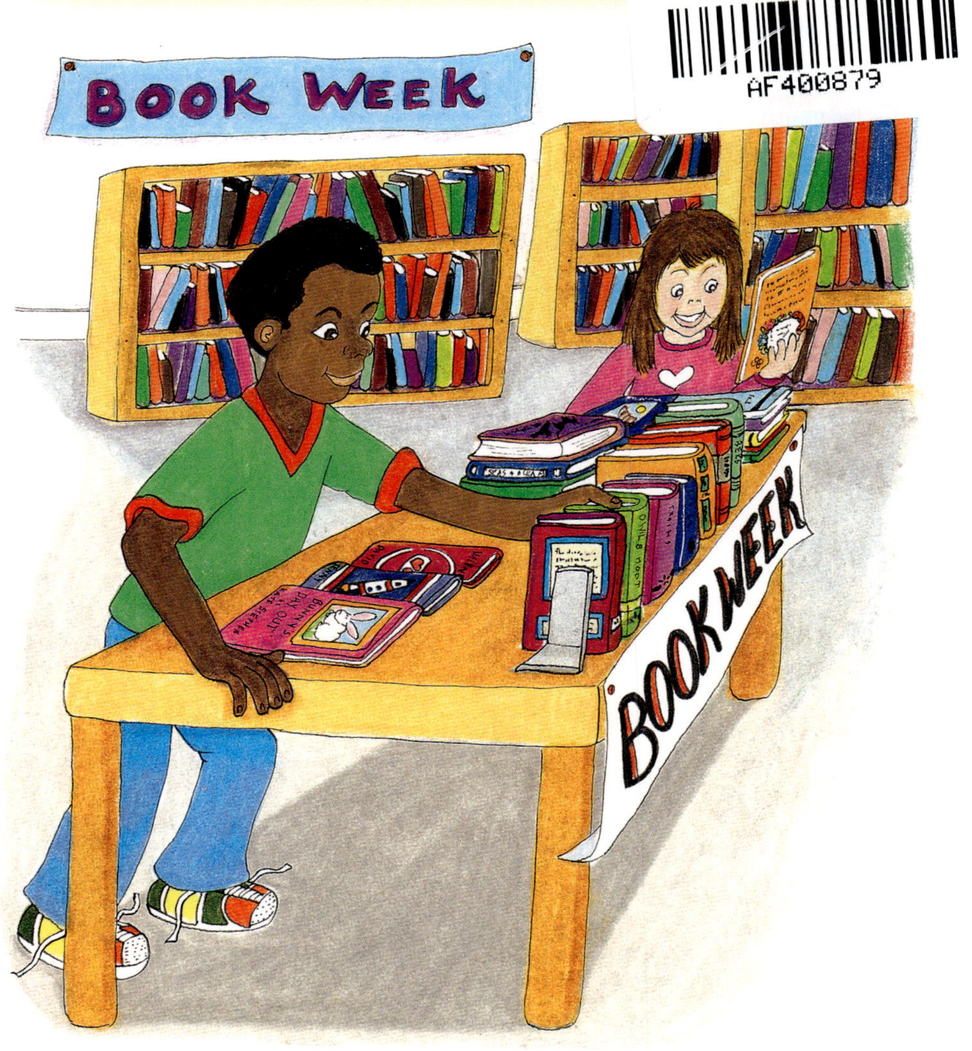

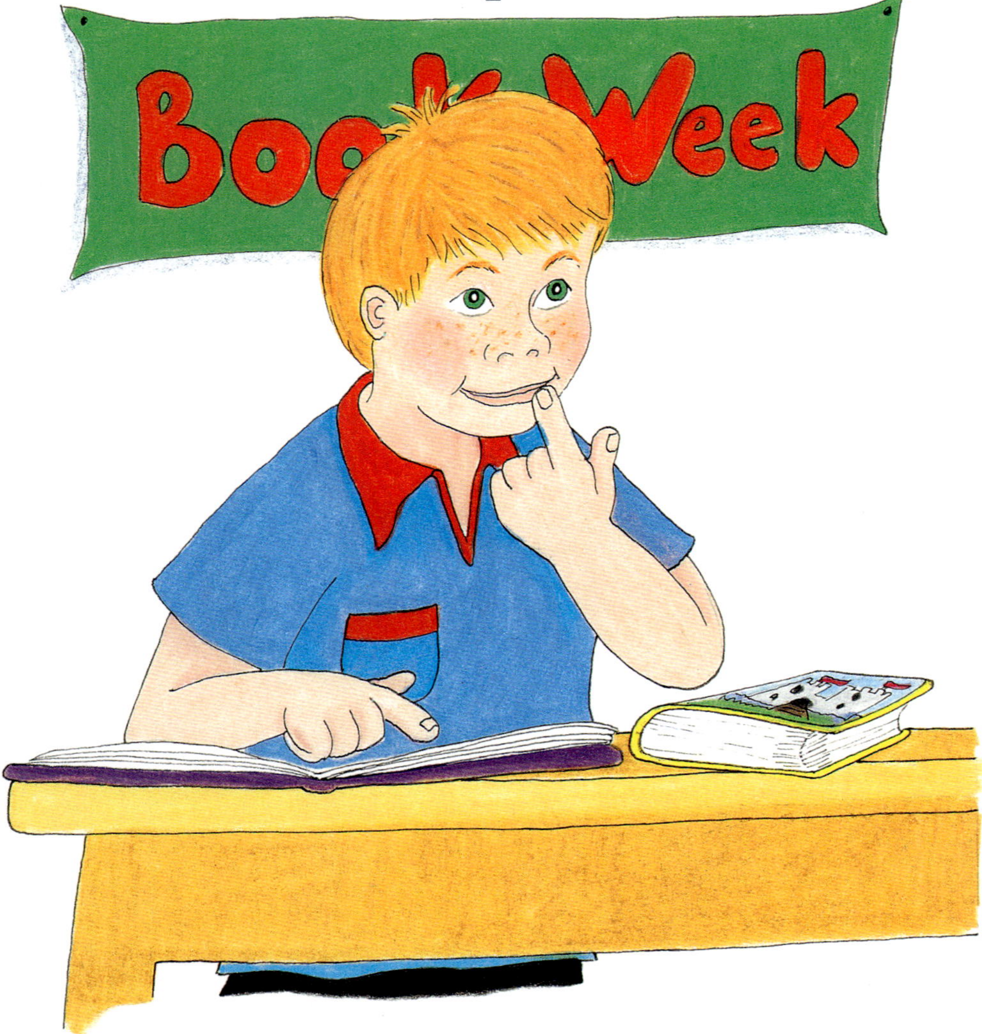

Gus had to dress up as a person from a book.

Adam was Jack

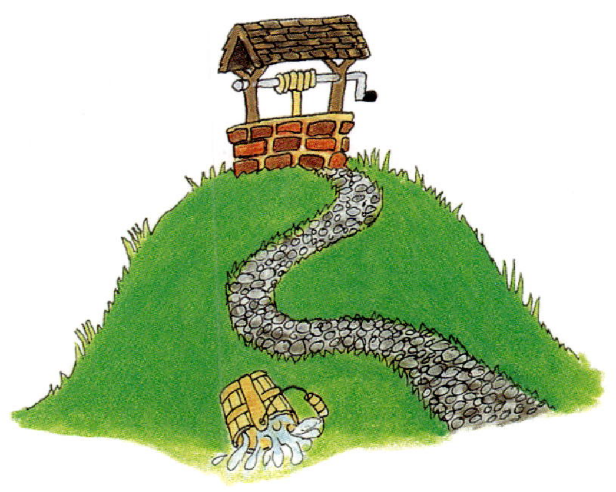

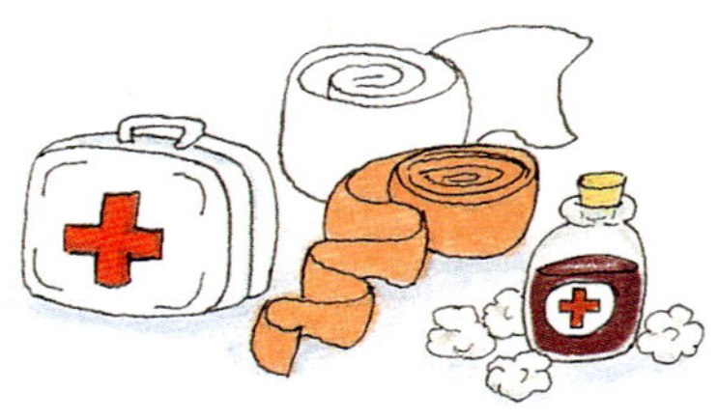

and Kim was Jill.

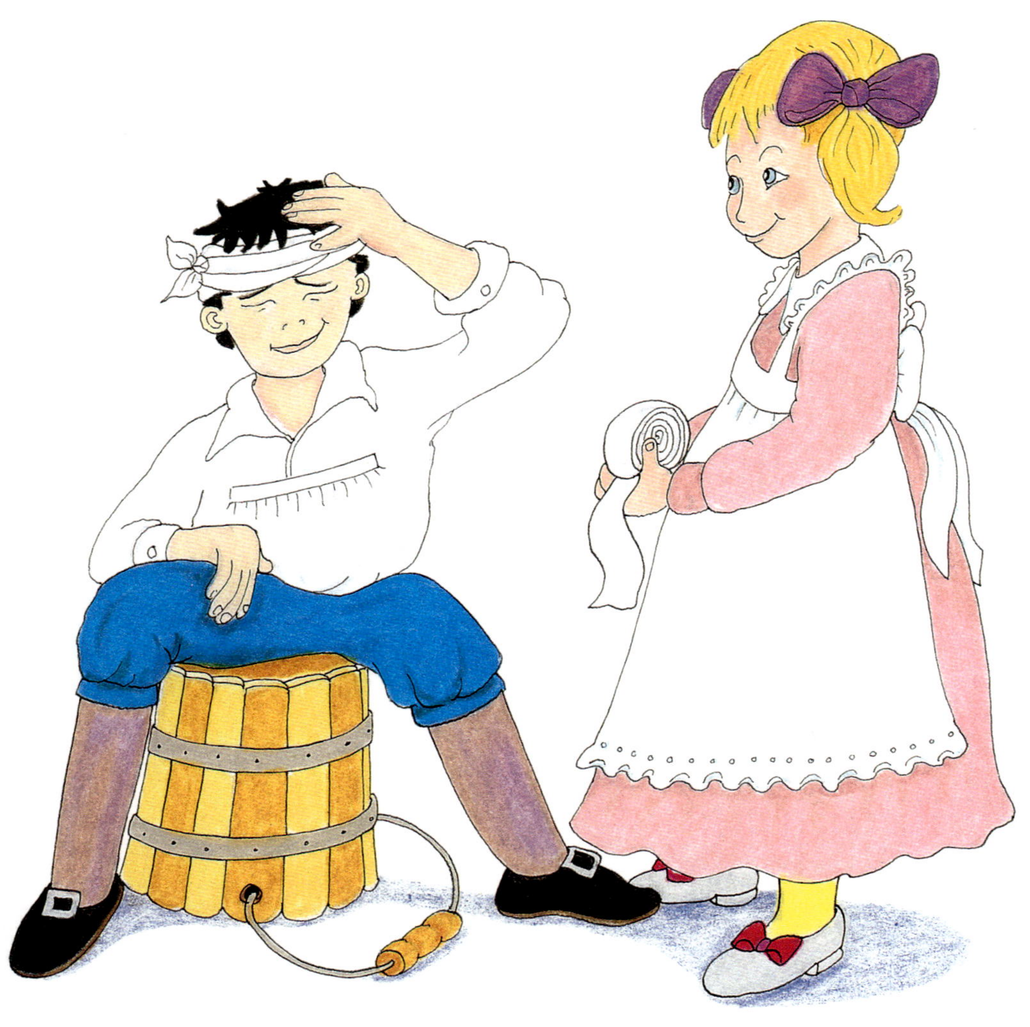

Jack

Jill

Hinda was Miss Muffet

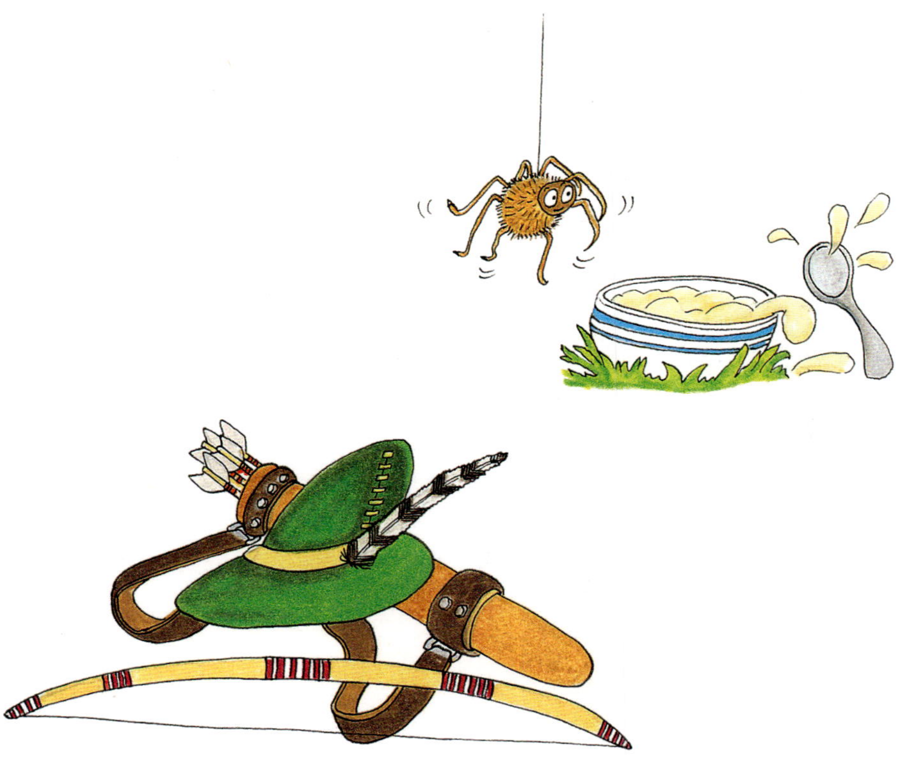

and Seth was Robin Hood.

Miss Muffet

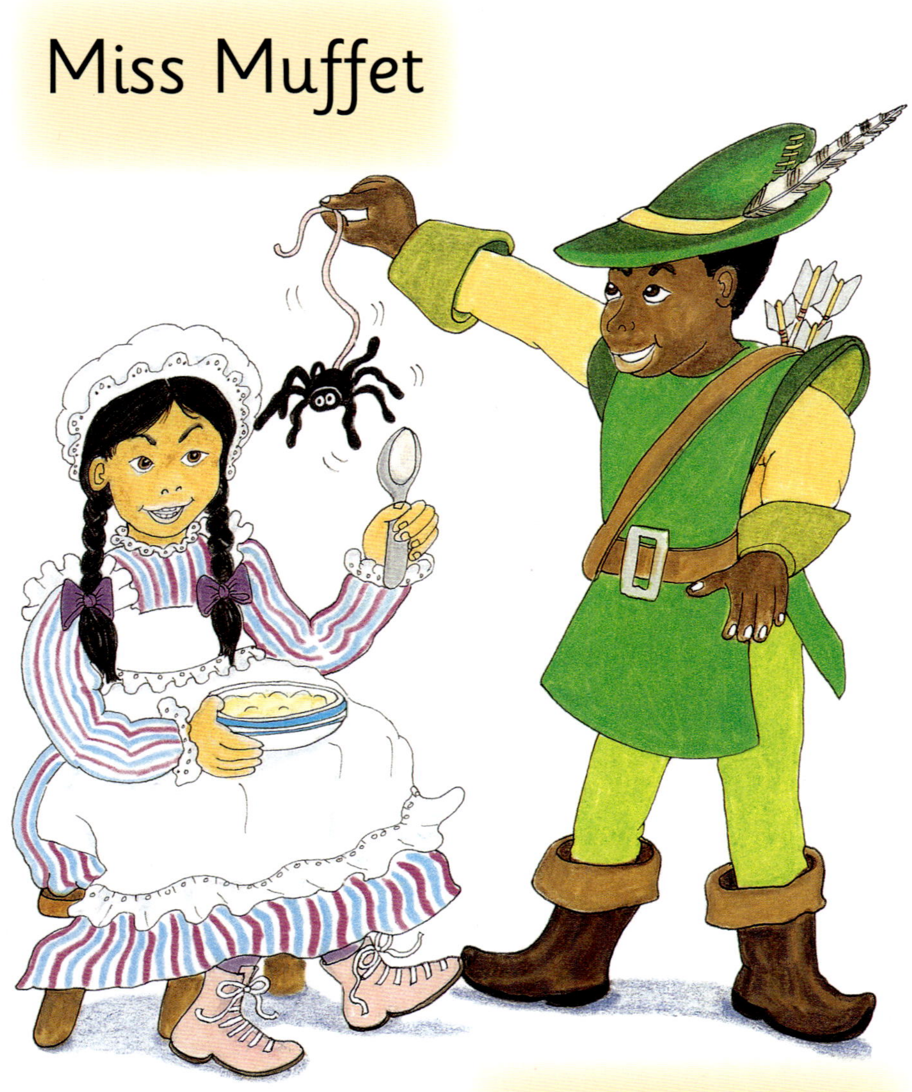

Robin Hood

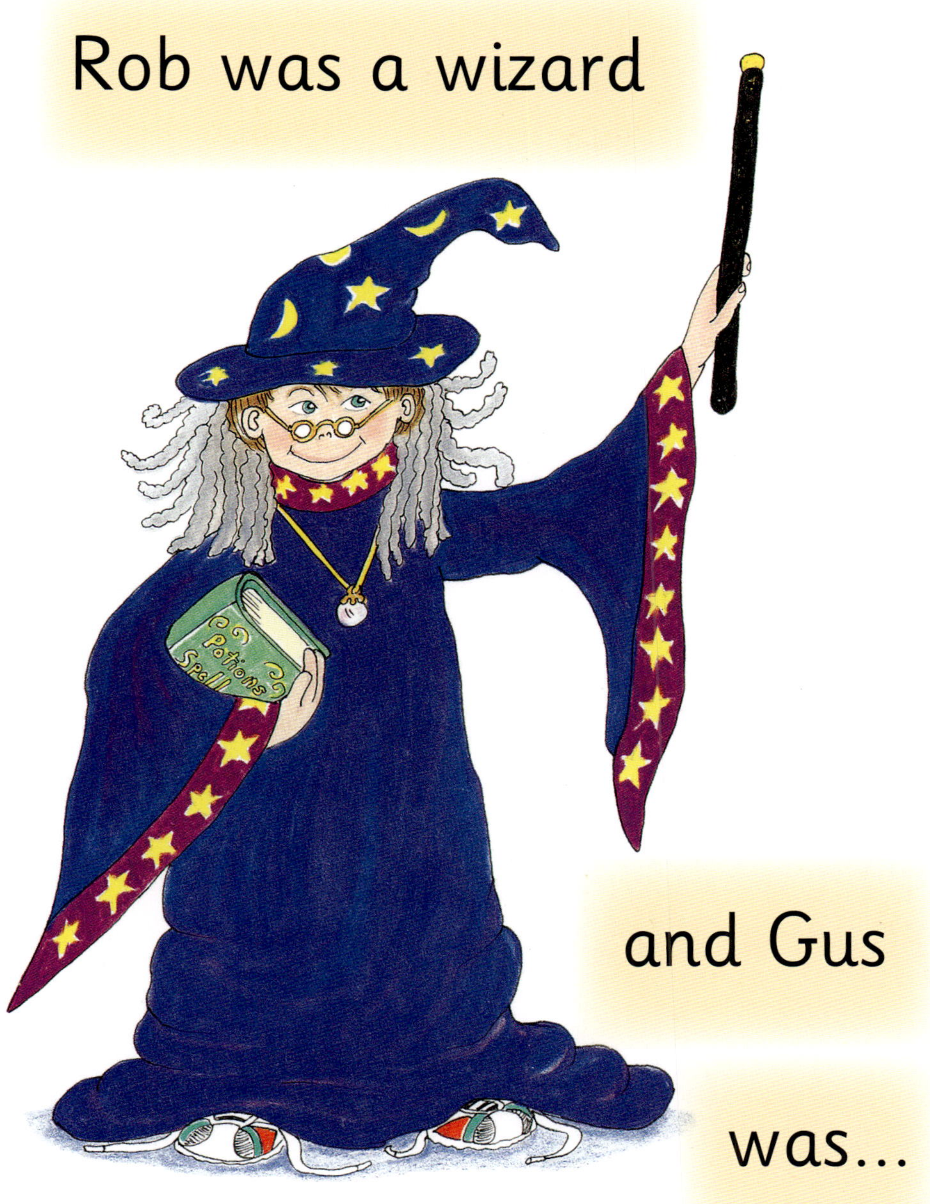

Rob was a wizard

and Gus

was...

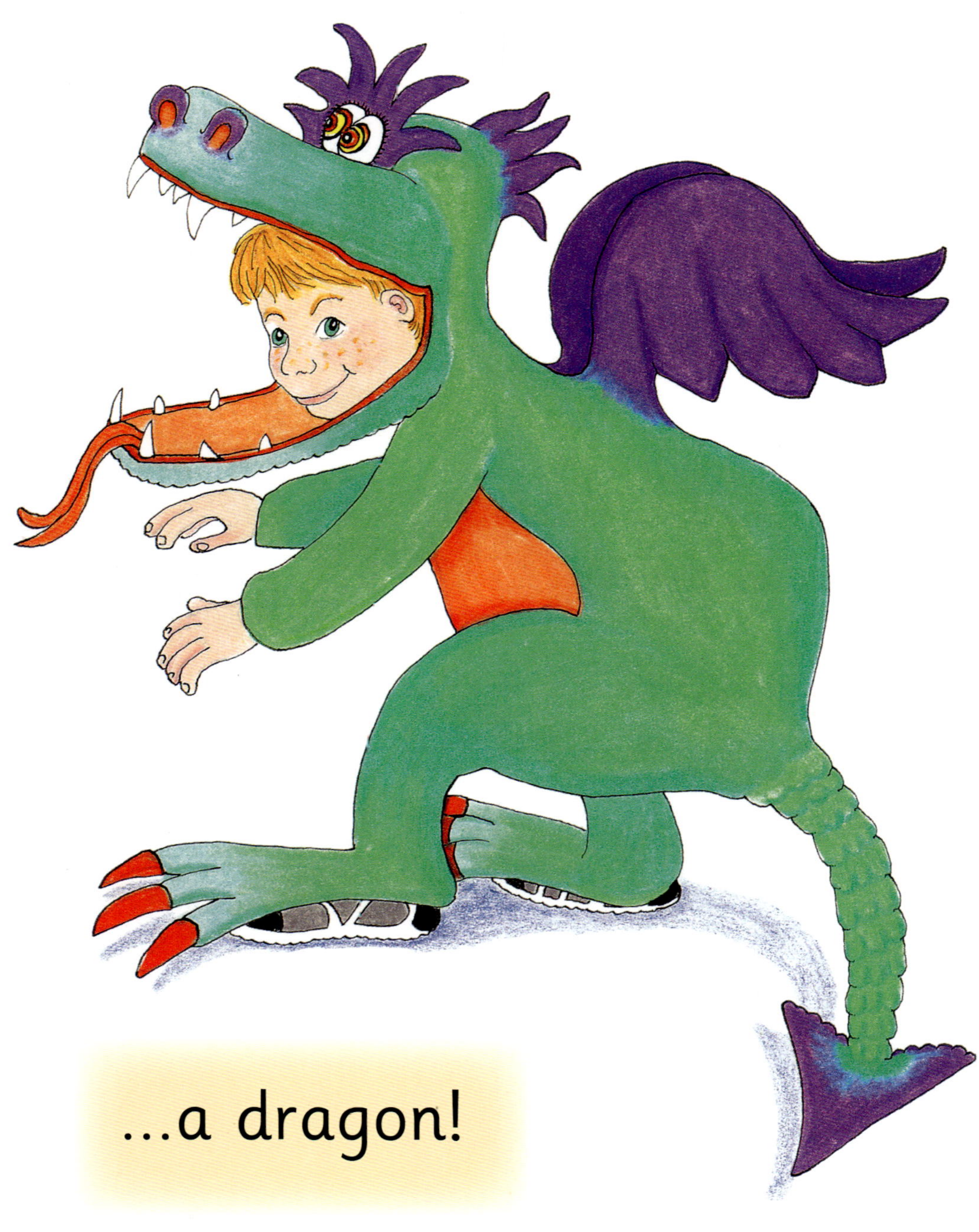

...a dragon!